To Tony with the hat
and Toni with the cat
—MM

PUFFIN BOOKS
Published by the Penguin Group
Penguin Books USA Inc., 375 Hudson Street, New York, New York 10014, U.S.A.
Penguin Books Ltd, 27 Wrights Lane, London W8 5TZ, England
Penguin Books Australia Ltd, Ringwood, Victoria, Australia
Penguin Books Canada Ltd, 10 Alcorn Avenue, Toronto, Ontario, Canada M4V 3B2
Penguin Books (N.Z.) Ltd, 182-190 Wairau Road, Auckland 10, New Zealand

Penguin Books Ltd, Registered Offices: Harmondsworth, Middlesex, England

First published in Great Britain by Hamish Hamilton Ltd, 1993
First published in the United States of America by Viking,
a division of Penguin Books USA Inc., 1993
Published in Puffin Books, 1995

1 3 5 7 9 10 8 6 4 2

Text copyright © Margaret Mahy, 1993
Illustrations copyright © Jonathan Allen, 1993
All rights reserved

THE LIBRARY OF CONGRESS HAS CATALOGED THE VIKING EDITION
UNDER CATALOG CARD NUMBER 92-61846.
ISBN 0-14-055331-2
Printed in China by Imago Publishing
A Vanessa Hamilton Book

MARGARET MAHY

The Three-Legged Cat

Illustrated by
Jonathan Allen

PUFFIN BOOKS

There was once an old tabby cat called Tom who longed to roam around the world. He longed to see hills and valleys, and wild, mysterious woods, as well. He longed to see the sea.

But Tom was a three-legged cat. Roaming was difficult with only three legs. What he was good at was curling up neatly, wrapping his tabby tail around himself, and going to sleep. As he slept, though, he dreamed of the wide world, and his three paws twitched.

Tom lived with shortsighted Mrs. Gimble of Number Seven, Cardamom Street. She was a very respectable widow. She liked cats, but she liked them best when they curled up and slept. It bothered her to see Tom come running, all hobbledy-bobbledy, whenever she opened the fridge.

"You'll eat me out of house and home," she said. She wanted a cat who would stay put and eat nothing. She certainly didn't want a roamer.

"One roamer in the family is quite enough," said Mrs. Gimble, for she had a rascally, roving drifter brother called Danny. All year he roamed uphill and down, and around the in-and-out edges of the world, wearing his revolting, molting Russian hat to keep his bald head warm. Once a year, he would come by Number Seven, Cardamom Street for a cup of tea and a chitchat. Oh, dear – Mrs. Gimble knew the neighbors would be watching as that revolting, molting Russian hat came up the street and turned in at her gate. "Yes," she grumbled to Tom. "One roamer is *more* than enough."

Tom wrapped himself around with his own tabby tail. He dreamed of roaming beside the sea. In his dream the sea was pink and fizzy. He dreamed of forests and fields of sheep. In his dream the forests were no higher than hedges, and the sheep ran about like woolly hedgehogs.

"Thank goodness Tom isn't one of those *roaming* cats," thought Mrs. Gimble. "I'm glad he has only three legs."

Then she heard a familiar step on the path. Horrakapotchkin! A molting, revolting Russian hat was coming up the path to her door. It was Danny the drifter. What would the neighbors say?

Knock, knock! went the door.

"Hello, Daisy! How about a cup of tea and a chitchat?" cried Danny.

"Oh, Danny, Danny! It's lovely to see you, but why don't you curl up and settle down?" Mrs. Gimble said. As she poured a cup of tea for her brother, she wept into the teapot.

"Don't cry into my tea, Daisy. I take sugar, not salt," said Danny. "But perhaps you're right. I love roaming the world, but my hat has molted badly. Somehow it doesn't keep my head as warm as it used to. It's not much fun roaming around with a bald head when it's cold. Perhaps I should settle down. Once more around the world, and then I'll think about it."

Mrs. Gimble was looking anxiously out of the window. Her neighbors didn't wander, but they did *whisper*. "Suppose they see there's a drifter sitting in here, having a cup of tea and a chitchat . . ." she thought. Hastily, she drew the curtains.

As Danny poured tea into his saucer (so that it would cool quickly), Mrs. Gimble told him all about a new furniture polish she had discovered in a sale. And Danny told her how to roam successfully during earthquakes. But Mrs. Gimble hated the idea of earthquakes, and Danny, who had no furniture, was not the least bit interested in furniture polish.

"Well, time to be on my way," Danny said, at last. He picked up his hat. But it wasn't his hat. He put on his hat. But it wasn't his hat. Out into the street he strolled, wearing Tom the three-legged cat, curled around his bald head, sound asleep.

"Good-bye, old girl," he called to Mrs. Gimble. "I'll be back this time next year for a cup of tea and a chitchat."

And off went Danny the drifter, and with him went Tom the three-
legged cat.

"My hat is deliciously warm," Danny thought, as he marched down the
road. "My bald head feels so cozy I could roam all the way around the world
wearing a hat as warm as this."

Tom the cat woke to find he was wrapped snugly around a bald head and riding down the road. There, right in front of him, was the beginning of the country. He saw hedges. He saw hogs. He even saw hedgehogs, and fields full of sheep. The world stretched all the way to the edge of the sky.

"I'm seeing the wide world at last," Tom thought in amazement. He wrapped his tabby tail more firmly around Danny's ears. "The wide world is so much wider than I thought it was."

"This hat is so much warmer than I thought it was," muttered Danny the drifter, walking up and over a hill.

Then Tom the cat saw the sea for the first time. It was not pink. It was green. It was not fizzy. It rolled backward and forward – all the way around the world.

"The sea! The sea!" thought Tom the cat. "I am seeing the sea." He began to purr.

"My hat is purring," thought Danny the drifter. "It's never purred before."

A tabby tail twitched in front of his eyes. "Horrakapotchkin! I've carried off Daisy's three-legged cat!" cried Danny the drifter. "It's just as well I have enough sausages for the two of us."

Meanwhile, back at Number Seven, Cardamom Street, Mrs. Gimble was sitting by the fire stroking the hat. It sat very still. And when she opened the fridge, the hat did not stir. It just sat there, molting slightly.

"My cat is suddenly cheap to feed," thought Mrs. Gimble. The hat did not show the least bit of interest, even when she ate her own fish dinner.

And out in the wide world Danny and Tom were sharing the sausages.
"I won't settle down after all," said Danny the drifter, stroking Tom.
"You can curl around my bald head and keep it cozy, while I do the
roaming for both of us. I've never had a better hat than a furry, friendly,
three-legged cat."

"And I've never had a better cat," said Mrs. Gimble, stroking the Russian hat tenderly. "It's true that it molts, but we all have our faults. And it's cheap to keep, and always asleep."

The wide world beckoned. Tom purred. The hat just sat on Mrs. Gimble's lap. And everyone lived happily ever after.